Dear Parent:
Your child's love of reading starts here!

Every child learns to read in a different way and at his or her own speed. Some go back and forth between reading levels and read favorite books again and again. Others read through each level in order. You can help your young reader improve and become more confident by encouraging his or her own interests and abilities. From books your child reads with you to the first books he or she reads alone, there are I Can Read Books for every stage of reading:

SHARED READING
Basic language, word repetition, and whimsical illustrations, ideal for sharing with your emergent reader

BEGINNING READING
Short sentences, familiar words, and simple concepts for children eager to read on their own

READING WITH HELP
Engaging stories, longer sentences, and language play for developing readers

READING ALONE
Complex plots, challenging vocabulary, and high-interest topics for the independent reader

I Can Read Books have introduced children to the joy of reading since 1957. Featuring award-winning authors and illustrators and a fabulous cast of beloved characters, I Can Read Books set the standard for beginning readers.

A lifetime of discovery begins with the magical words "I Can Read!"

Visit www.icanread.com for information
on enriching your child's reading experience.

Pete the Cat Saves Up
Text copyright © 2023 by Kimberly Dean and James Dean
Illustrations copyright © 2023 by James Dean
Pete the Cat is a registered trademark of Pete the Cat, LLC.
www.icanread.com

Library of Congress Control Number: 2022946540
ISBN 978-0-06-297437-2 (trade bdg.)—ISBN 978-0-06-297436-5 (pbk.)

Book design by Marisa Rother
23 24 25 26 27 LB   10 9 8 7 6 5 4 3 2 1   First Edition

I Can Read!

BEGINNING **1** READING

Pete the Cat

SAVES UP

TOY SALE

SHARKBOT

by Kimberly & James Dean

HARPER

An Imprint of HarperCollinsPublishers

Pete the Cat loves the toy store!

There are so many groovy things,

like the new robot shark toy.

It's the coolest!

Pete really wants a Sharkbot!

But Pete didn't bring any money.

At home, Pete checks his bank.

It's almost empty!

He does not have enough money

to buy a Sharkbot.

Pete thinks of ideas

for how to earn money

so he can buy a Sharkbot.

Pete looks out the window.

It's snowing!

He knows what to do!

Pete shovels snow for his neighbors.

"Great job!" says Grumpy Toad's dad.

He pays Pete for his work.

"Thank you!" Pete says.

Pete thinks about buying hot cocoa.

But he saves his money.

He will make hot cocoa at home.

Pete counts his money.

It's not enough to buy a Sharkbot.

That's okay.

He puts the money in his bank.

"What can I do next?" he thinks.

Then the snow melts.

Mom offers to pay Pete

if he helps her plant flowers.

"You did a great job, Pete!"

Mom says.

Mom pays Pete for his work.

Pete thinks about buying a ticket
for the movies.
But Pete saves his money.
He will watch a movie at home.

Pete counts his money.

"Getting closer!" Pete says.

He puts the money in his bank.

It's very hot outside.

Pete knows what to do!

He sets up a lemonade stand.

18

Everyone shows up to buy
a cup of cold lemonade.
"Yummy!" says Gus.

Pete hears the ice cream truck.

He thinks about buying an ice pop.

But Pete saves his money.

He will eat one from the freezer.

Pete counts his money.

"Almost there!" Pete says.

He puts his money in the bank.

When summer ends, Pete has saved
almost enough to buy a Sharkbot.
He's so close!

He rakes leaves for Grandma.

"Awesome!" Grandma says,

and pays Pete for his work.

Pete thinks about buying

a spooky mask for Halloween.

But Pete saves his money.

He makes his own spooky mask!

24

Pete puts his money in his bank.

The bank looks full!

"Wow!" Pete says.

Pete counts the money in his bank.

He has saved enough money to buy

a Sharkbot!

"Yay!" Pete cheers.

Mom, Dad, and Bob cheer too.

"Great job saving up!" they say.

The next day, Pete brings his money to the toy store.

Pete hands his money to the clerk.

The clerk hands Pete

his new Sharkbot toy.

SHARKBOT

Pete loves his Sharkbot!

But now Pete really wants

a Rocket Racer

for his Sharkbot to ride.

Pete does not have enough money

for the Rocket Racer.

But he knows what to do!

Saving up is cool!